Romulus and Remus

Mick Gowar and Andrew Breakspeare

FRANKLIN WATTS

To Sam – M.G.

Chapter 1:
Brothers

Many years ago in the city of Alba Longa, there lived a king called Numitor. King Numitor had a daughter, Princess Rhea Silvia, who had just given birth to twin boys. She called them Romulus and Remus.

Numitor couldn't wait to show off his grandsons. "These boys will be kings of Alba Longa after me," he said, proudly. He gave them each a gold necklace to show everyone that the two boys were his heirs.

But not everyone was happy. Numitor had a younger brother called Amulius who was jealous of Numitor, and he was jealous of the two baby princes, too.

Amulius always thought he would be king after Numitor died. He was furious when he heard about the twins. "Now I'll never be king," he thought, "unless I get rid of those boys." Amulius called on all his soldier friends to help him and they burst into the palace of King Numitor.

"I'm the king now!" Amulius told his
brother. "This is my palace. Leave at once!"
Then Amulius sent for Romulus and Remus,
to make sure they would never be kings
instead of him.

A river flowed past the palace. Amulius
put Romulus and Remus in a basket. He
took the basket down to the river bank and
pushed it out into the deep waters. As the
basket floated away, Amulius smiled and
said to himself, "Now I really am the king!"

Chapter 2:
Mother Wolf,
Father Woodpecker

The little basket sped down the river, but
when it came to a bend it hit the river bank.
The basket tipped over and out onto the
grass tumbled the twins.

A she-wolf heard the babies crying.
She rolled them onto their blanket and
gently carried them back to her den
under a fig tree.

High in the fig tree lived a woodpecker.
Every day the wolf would give the twins
her milk to drink, and the woodpecker
would drop ripe figs from the tree for the
two boys to eat.

But Romulus and Remus did not like
to share their food. As they grew
older they quarrelled and fought:
"The figs are mine!" cried Romulus.
"No, they're mine!" shouted Remus.

The she-wolf and the woodpecker
had no way to stop the boys
fighting each other.

One day, a shepherd heard the twins fighting and came to find out what the noise was. Thinking they meant to harm the babies, he chased the she-wolf and the woodpecker away.

Then he carried the twins back to his cottage. "I will look after you as if you were my own sons," he told Romulus and Remus.

Chapter 3:
Return to Alba Longa

When they were sixteen years old, Romulus and Remus decided to walk to Alba Longa to see what the city was like. Neither of them could remember the palace where they had once been princes. They couldn't even remember Princess Rhea Silvia, their mother.

But one of King Numitor's ministers saw the gold necklaces and immediately knew who the two boys were.

"Come with me, quickly," he whispered. "Your grandfather, King Numitor has been in hiding. He needs your help."

The boys were reunited with their grandfather.

Numitor told the twins who they were, and
what had happened sixteen years before.
"I'll help you!" cried Romulus grabbing
a sword.
"So will I!" shouted Remus seizing a spear.
Romulus and Remus went to the palace
with Numitor.

"You're not the true king of Alba Longa!"
said Romulus.
"Our grandfather, Numitor, is the true king
of Alba Longa," said Remus.
Amulius was shocked. He believed the twins
had drowned all those years ago. There was
a terrible fight and Amulius was killed.

Numitor was king once again. There was a great banquet at the palace to celebrate. The people of Alba Longa brought gifts: golden cups for the king to drink from, bottles of the finest wines for the king to drink, rolls of the finest silks to make royal robes for the king to wear.

But Romulus and Remus started to quarrel. "I should sit next to grandfather," cried Romulus. "I'm going to be king of Alba Longa after him."

"No you're not!" shouted Remus. "I'm going to be king of Alba Longa after him!"

"Won't!"

"Will!"

"Why don't you build a new city?" said King
Numitor. "Then you can both be kings."
"I will be the greatest king!" said Romulus.
"Never!" said Remus.

Chapter 4:
The New City

"We should build our city on that hill," said Romulus pointing to the north.

"No," said Remus. "We should build our city on that hill," and he pointed to the south.

"My hill!" cried Romulus.

"No, mine!" shouted Remus.

Romulus harnessed two oxen to a plough, and ploughed a huge circle in the dirt on the side of his hill.

"Look, Remus!" he called to his brother. "This is my city wall!"

Remus sneered. "It's not a wall it's just a ditch!" And he jumped over it. "Hah!"

Romulus picked up a rock. "Apologise, or…"

"Or what?" said Remus.

Romulus threw the rock with all his strength. It struck Remus on the head. He fell to the ground, dead. Remus was buried on the hillside where he wanted to build his city.

Romulus summoned the people from the fields and farms all around. "I am the king of this new city," said Romulus. "Everyone who helps me build my city can live safely behind its strong walls, travel along its long straight roads, and buy food, drink and clothes from its shops. I will call the city Rome – after myself: Romulus.

"Everyone who lives in my city will be my people: Romans. And one day it will be the greatest city in the whole world."

The people of Rome saw how Romulus's eyes shone when he spoke about his city. So they all cheered, to show how happy they were to have a new king and to be Romans.

But the she-wolf and the woodpecker and the shepherd were sad. Every time they saw Romulus's wonderful new city, they thought of poor Remus and of the quarrels between the brothers, Numitor and Amulius, and Romulus and Remus.

About the story

The story of *Romulus and Remus* has been famous for more than 2000 years. It is said that Romulus founded Rome in 753 BCE, and that the foundation story was well known in the fourth century BCE. By 269 BCE, the image of the she-wolf and the twins appears on one of the first Roman coins. There are many different versions. In one version, Remus is said to have lived and founded a city called Remuria five miles away from Rome! The story was written down by Diocles, a historian from the late 4th, early third century BCE. His works have been lost but we know about them through other writers. The Greek scholar Plutarch acknowledges Diocles in his biography *Lives.*

Be in the story!

Imagine you are King Numitor and you are seeing the twins for the first time since they were babies. What will you say to them?

Now imagine you are Amulius. How do you feel when the twins turn up with your brother all these years later?

First published in 2014 by
Franklin Watts
338 Euston Road
London
NW1 3BH

Franklin Watts Australia
Level 17/207 Kent Street
Sydney
NSW 2000

A CIP catalogue record for this book is available
from the British Library.

The artwork for this story first appeared in
Hopscotch Myths: Romulus and Remus

ISBN 978 1 4451 3385 0 (hbk)
ISBN 978 1 4451 3386 7 (pbk)
ISBN 978 1 4451 3388 1 (library ebook)
ISBN 978 1 4451 3387 4 (ebook)

Series Editor: Jackie Hamley
Series Advisor: Catherine Glavina
Series Designer: Cathryn Gilbert

Printed in China

Franklin Watts is a divison of
Hachette Children's Books,
an Hachette UK company.
www.hachette.co.uk